# MY AWESOME BALI ADVENTURE

JUMP ONLINE TO UNLOCK EVEN MORE FUN STUFF TO DO AT WWW.KIDDING-AROUND.ORG

WRITTEN BY PHILLIP GWYNNE & ELIZA MCCANN

ART & DESIGN BY TINNE CORNELISSEN
CORNELISSEN.TINNE@GMAIL.COM

PUBLISHED BY KIDDING AROUND
WWW.KIDDING-AROUND.ORG
INFO@KIDDING-AROUND.ORG

ISBN 978-0-646-91800-6

# LET'S MAKE THIS BOOK YOUR OWN

WHAT'S YOUR NAME?

DATE OF BIRTH?

PASSPORT NUMBER?

DRAW YOUR PASSPORT PHOTO

JUST IN CASE YOUR BOOK GETS LOST... WHAT IS YOUR HOME ADDRESS?

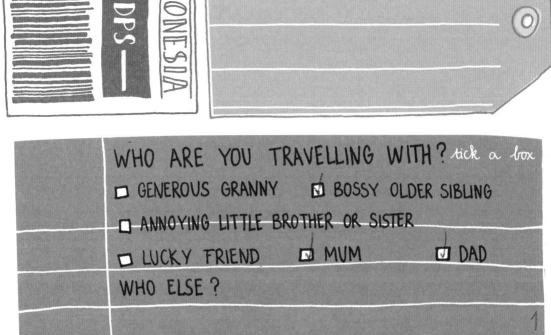

INDONESIA

DPS

WHO ARE YOU TRAVELLING WITH? *tick a box*

☐ GENEROUS GRANNY      ☑ BOSSY OLDER SIBLING

☐ ANNOYING LITTLE BROTHER OR SISTER

☐ LUCKY FRIEND      ☑ MUM      ☑ DAD

WHO ELSE?

1

# COLOUR IN THIS PLANE SO IT'S JUST LIKE YOURS !

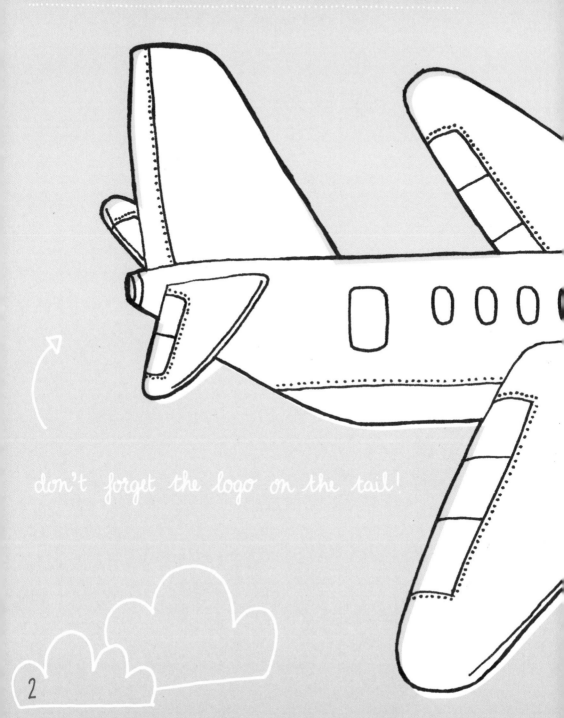

don't forget the logo on the tail!

3

# GETTING THERE

WHAT AIRPORT DID YOU LEAVE FROM?

..............................................................

HOW DID YOU GET TO THE AIRPORT?

..............................................................

HOW LONG WAS THE FLIGHT?

*hours* ___ *minutes*

WHAT SEAT WERE YOU IN?

..............................................................

DID YOU LUCK OUT AND GET THE WINDOW SEAT?

☑ *yes*  ☐ *no*

WHO DID YOU SIT NEXT TO?

..............................................................

..............................................................

WAS THE FLIGHT ?

☐ BORING
☐ BUMPY
☑ FUN! I watched movies and played games

WHAT MOVIES DID YOU WATCH?

.......................................................................................

.......................................................................................

WHAT GAMES DID YOU PLAY?

.......................................................................................

.......................................................................................

MY FAVOURITE FOOD I ATE ON THE PLANE WAS...

.......................................................................................

.......................................................................................

# HAVE YOU BEEN TO BALI BEFORE ?

YES (lucky you!)

NO

WHAT DO YOU THINK BALI WILL BE LIKE?

...................................................................

...................................................................

...................................................................

HOW MANY TIMES ?

☐ ONCE

☐ TWICE

☐ BANYAK
(which is Indonesian for many!)

☐ ONLY WHEN I WAS A BABY, I DON'T REMEMBER

WRITE DOWN YOUR BME (Best Memory Ever) FROM YOUR LAST TIME IN BALI!

...................................................................

...................................................................

WHAT ARE YOU REALLY LOOKING FORWARD TO DOING AGAIN IN BALI?

...................................................................

...................................................................

STICK IN YOUR BOARDING PASS OR MAYBE DRAW SOME PICTURES.
HERE ARE SOME SUGGESTIONS... YOUR FAVOURITE FLIGHT ATTENDANT,
THE BEST THING YOU SAW FROM THE WINDOW OR EVEN YOUR INFLIGHT MEAL!

Clouds are cool...

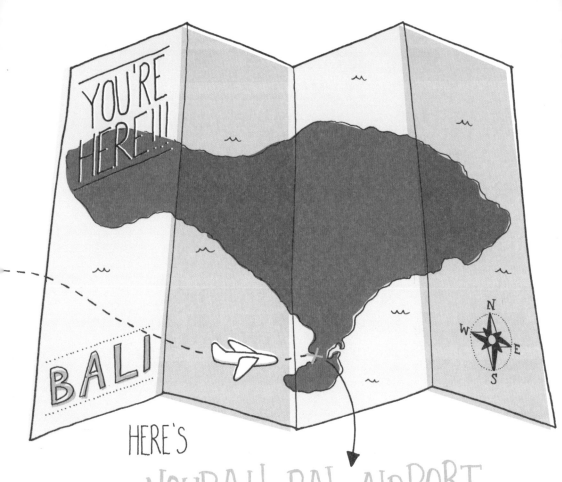

HERE'S

NGURAH RAI AIRPORT

YOUR FIRST PORT OF CALL.

DID YOU GET A STAMP IN YOUR PASSPORT? ☑ *yes*  ☐ *no*

HERE'S TWO PASSPORTS THAT WERE STAMPED.
CAN YOU SPOT THE **5** DIFFERENCES?

9

WHO PICKED YOU UP FROM THE AIRPORT? Daniel .....................................................

................................................................................................

HOW LONG WAS THE DRIVE TO THE HOTEL OR VILLA? 1 hours 30 minutes

DRAW A PICTURE OF YOUR FAMILY IN THE CAR!
  OR YOU CAN GO BALI STYLE AND PUT EVERYONE ON ONE MOTORBIKE.

         not much room for the suitcases!

HEY!!! ALWAYS WEAR A HELMET WHEN YOU GET ON A MOTORBIKE! ALWAYS!!!

# WHAT DO YOU IMMEDIATELY NOTICE THAT IS DIFFERENT FROM HOME?!

Sights, smells and sounds.....

## ☀ SIGHTS ☀

SMELLS

WHAT ABOUT DIFFERENT SOUNDS? DO YOU HEAR THE CONSTANT
BRRROOOOOMMM OF MOTORBIKES?

# 👂 SOUNDS 👂

IF YOU SPOT ANY OF THESE, GIVE THEM A TICK!

☑ RICE PADDY

☑ BUDDHA STATUE

☑ COCONUT TREE

☑ BAKSO CART

16

AND IF YOU WANT, YELL OUT 'BALI SPOTTO!'

☐ BINTANG SINGLET

☑ STREET SIGN TO DENPASAR

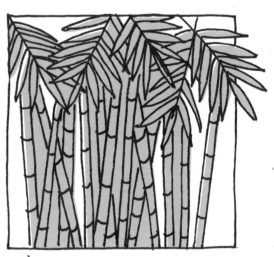

☑ BAMBOO PLANT

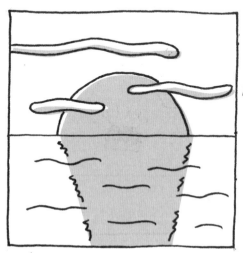

☑ AN AMAZING SUNSET

☐ 'HATI HATI' SIGN

('HATI HATI' MEANS 'CAREFUL' IN BAHASA INDONESIA)

☐ DOG ON A MOTORBIKE

☑ OFFERING IN THE MIDDLE OF AN INTERSECTION

☑ MONKEY

☑ FOUR PEOPLE ON
   A MOTORBIKE

☑ BALI COW

☑ FRANGIPANI TREE

☑ SARONG

# MY AWESOME BALI SPOTTO

NOW IT'S TIME TO CREATE YOUR VERY OWN SPOTTO! *let's see what you come up with...*

# MONEY, MONEY, MONEY.............

HAVE YOU ALWAYS WANTED TO BE A MILLIONAIRE? THERE ARE LOTS OF ZEROES WITH THE RUPIAH. HERE'S A LIST OF THE NOTES YOU'LL FIND...

CAN YOU FIND OUT WHAT EACH NOTE IS WORTH? FILL IN THE MISSING NUMBERS.

**5000** WILL BUY YOU an ice cream

**10 000** WILL BUY YOU A DELICIOUSLY REFRESHING COCONUT AT A ROADSIDE STALL

**50 000** WILL BUY YOU A SARONG OR EVEN A PAIR OF SUNGLASSES

**100 000** WILL BUY YOU 4 nasi gorengs AT A WARUNG

23

HANUMAN, THE WHITE MONKEY, IS ONE OF BALI'S MOST LOVED GODS, AND MANY STORIES ARE TOLD OF HIS AWESOME ADVENTURES.

BELIEVING IT TO BE A RIPE MANGO, HE ONCE TRIED TO EAT THE SUN!

HANUMAN WAS ALSO VERY NAUGHTY WHEN HE WAS YOUNG, USING HIS SUPERNATURAL POWERS TO PESTER THE WISE MEN LIVING IN THE FOREST - HE CREATED A WHIRLWIND WITH HIS BREATH, PUT OUT THEIR SACRED FIRES, HE EVEN PULLED THEIR BEARDS! HAVE A GO AT WRITING YOUR VERY OWN HANUMAN STORY ON THE FOLLOWING PAGES...

(maybe you could ask a Balinese
 person to tell you more about
 their mischievous monkey god)

# HANUMAN, THE MISCHIEVOUS WHITE MONKEY.

AN ORIGINAL STORY BY ...................................................................................................................

# PSSSTTT... PERMISI... EXCUSE ME.

WANT TO LEARN SOME BAHASA INDONESIA? LET'S START WITH NUMBERS

HERE ARE SOME REALLY HANDY WORDS TO KNOW IN BAHASA

*permisi*
-EXCUSE ME

KIRI
-LEFT

*kanan*
-RIGHT

-HOT
PANAS

*dingin*
-COLD

BANYAK
– MANY

Sedikit
– A FEW

BAGUS
– GOOD

TERIMA KASIH
– THANK YOU

TIDAK APA APA
– NO PROBLEMS

31

## YOUR BAHASA

DID YOU LEARN ANY OTHER AWESOME WORDS THAT YOU WANT TO REMEMBER?
YOU CAN IMPRESS YOUR FRIENDS BACK HOME OR REMEMBER THEM FOR WHEN
YOU COME BACK - KEMBALI - TO BALI! WE'LL START YOU OFF...

| BAHASA | ENGLISH |
|--------|---------|
| pintar | clever |
|  |  |
|  |  |
|  |  |
|  |  |
|  |  |
|  |  |
|  |  |

# BAHASA

# ENGLISH

# BALINESE MASKS

FOR THOUSANDS OF YEARS BALINESE HAVE BEEN CARVING MASKS.
THEY ARE CALLED 'TOPENG'. *colour in this one.*

34

# WEATHER

IN BALI IT'S PRETTY MUCH HOT ALL YEAR ROUND.

CAN YOU GUESS THE AVERAGE TEMPERATURE?

☐ 24 - 29 degrees celsius
☑ 29 - 32 degrees celsius
☐ 32 - 36 degrees celsius

THE SEASONS IN BALI LOOK A LITTLE SOMETHING LIKE THIS....

DO YOU KNOW THE RAINIEST MONTH IN BALI? ...................................................................

DO YOU KNOW THE DRIEST MONTH? ...........................................................

UNDER THE SEA IF YOU THOUGHT BALI WAS COOL ON LAND, WAIT TILL YOU PUT ON YOUR MASK AND FINS AND CHECK OUT WHAT'S UNDER THE SEA. IT REALLY IS A GREAT PLACE TO SNORKEL AND DIVE.

36

37

# SURFING

BALI IS FAMOUS FOR ITS SURF, AND SOME OF ITS MOST WELL KNOWN BREAKS ARE KUTA, CANGGU, PADANG PADANG AND – IF YOU'RE REALLY BRAVE – ULUWATU. EPIC!

COLOUR IN THIS BOARD WITH YOUR OWN DESIGN.

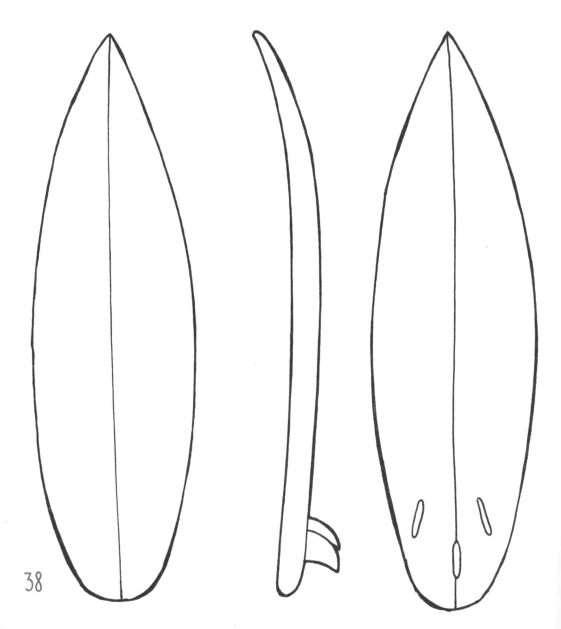

38

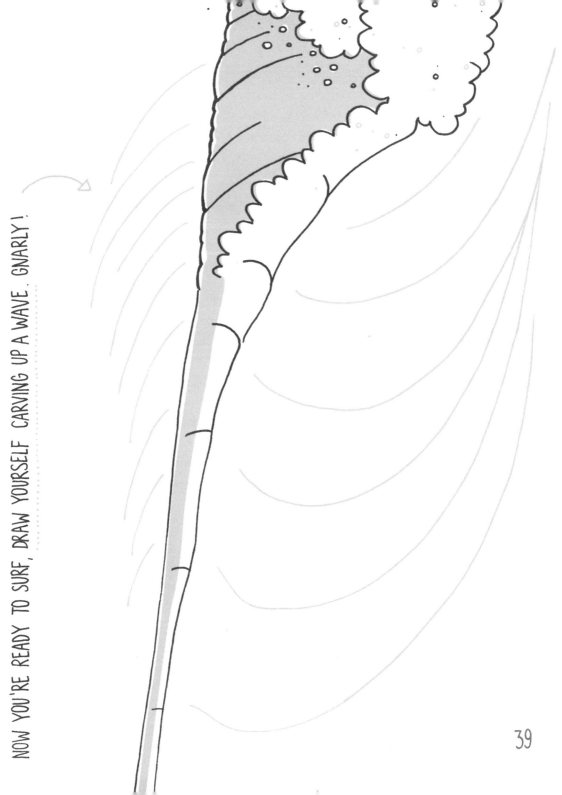

NOW YOU'RE READY TO SURF, DRAW YOURSELF CARVING UP A WAVE. GNARLY!

# ACROSS

1&3 THESE ARE PARADED THE NIGHT BEFORE NYEPI (4, 4)
6 AN ISLAND IN INDONESIA (4)
(clue: you're probably here now!)
7 'SHADOW PUPPET' IN BAHASA- WAYANG ____ (5)
9 ALSO KNOWN AS CANANG. THIS IS PRESENTED TO THE GODS (8)
12 HINDU CHANT (2)
13 'CRAZY' IN BAHASA (4)
14 THESE FLY IN THE SKY DURING THE DRY SEASON (5)

# DOWN

2 'SUGAR' IN BAHASA (4)
4 BALINESE ORCHESTRA (7)
5 THERE ARE LOTS OF THESE FLYING AROUND AT NIGHT IN BALI (4)
6 WELL KNOWN DANCE IN BALI (6)
8 THE BALINESE MONKEY DANCE (5)
10 WOVEN FABRIC IN INDONESIA (4)
11 THE HINDU RELIGION HAS MANY OF THESE (4)

40

BALI IS ONE OF THE MANY - OVER 18,000! - ISLANDS THAT MAKE UP INDONESIA.

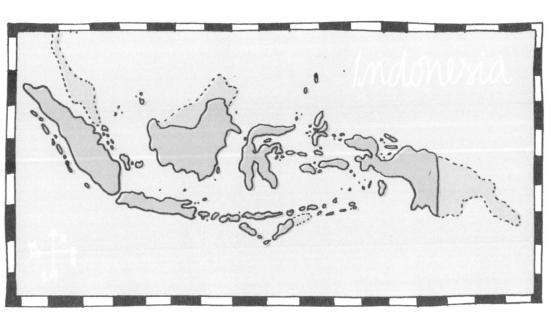

DRAW A LINE TO EACH OF THESE ISLANDS ON THE MAP

FLORES   LOMBOK   SUMATRA

SULAWESI   BALI

SUMBAWA

JAVA   KALIMANTAN

# FOOD

HERE ARE SOME GOOD WORDS TO KNOW:

MAKANAN
- FOOD

- HUNGRY
LAPAR

- DRINK
MINUMAN

HAUS
- THIRSTY

ENAK
- DELICIOUS

- REALLY DELICIOUS
ENAK SEKALI

# ARE YOU GOING OUT FOR DINNER WITH THE FAMILY?
## HERE ARE SOME PHRASES IN BAHASA THAT MIGHT COME IN HANDY...

### MAKANAN INI PEDAS?
IS THIS SPICY?

### BOLEH MINTA DUA SENDOK ES KRIM?
CAN I PLEASE HAVE 2 SCOOPS OF ICE CREAM?

### BOLEH MINTA LAGI?
CAN I HAVE SOME MORE PLEASE?

### IBU DAN AYAH YANG AKAN MEMBAYAR.
MUM AND DAD WILL PAY FOR THAT!

HERE ARE SOME FAMOUS INDONESIAN DISHES.
HAVE YOU TRIED ANY OF THESE YET?

☐ SOTO AYAM
(CHICKEN NOODLE SOUP)

☐ NASI GORENG
(FRIED RICE)

☐ CHICKEN SATAY

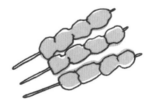

☐ MIE GORENG
(FRIED NOODLES)

☐ CHICKEN NUGGETS
(only joking)

# WHAT HAS BEEN YOUR FAVOURITE FOOD IN BALI?
write them down so you don't forget!

..................................................................................................................

..................................................................................................................

..................................................................................................................

..................................................................................................................

..................................................................................................................

..................................................................................................................

..................................................................................................................

..................................................................................................................

..................................................................................................................

..................................................................................................................

..................................................................................................................

# FRUIT

THERE IS SO MUCH DELICIOUS FRUIT IN BALI. WHICH ONES HAVE YOU TRIED?
RATE THEM FROM 1 - *yuck* TO 10 - *totally delicious* COLOUR THEM IN, TOO.

6 WATERMELON

4 PAPAYA

6 PINEAPPLE

6 Salak

RAMBUTAN

5

9 MANGO

46

mangosteen 7

Guava 2

banana 7

STARFRUIT 5

DURIAN

WHAT IS YOUR FAVOURITE FRUIT TO EAT IN BALI?

# SHHHHHHHHHHHHHHH!!!!!!!!!!!

BE VERY, VERY QUIET. EVERY YEAR BALI HAS A DAY OF SILENCE CALLED NYEPI.
THE AIRPORT IS CLOSED. YOU CAN'T DRIVE YOUR CAR OR MOTORBIKE
AND NO LIGHTS CAN BE TURNED ON. EVERYTHING IS SILENT.

DO YOU KNOW WHY?
BECAUSE THE BALINESE WANT TO MAKE THE BAD SPIRITS THINK THAT NO ONE IS HOME
ON THE ISLAND. BUT THE NIGHT BEFORE NYEPI IS ANYTHING BUT QUIET. BALINESE WANT T
SCARE THE BAD SPIRITS AWAY SO THAT'S WHEN THE OGOH-OGOHS COME OUT!

IF YOU THOUGHT HALLOWEEN WAS SCARY, THINK AGAIN!

now draw the

# SCARIEST, UGLIEST and GROSSEST

ogoh - ogoh you can!

HERE'S YOUR CHANCE TO TRY AGAIN. SEE IF YOU CAN FIND THE NUMBERS SATU TO SEPULUH...
THAT'S ONE TO TEN IN CASE YOU'VE FORGOTTEN.

**SATU**

**DUA**

**TIGA**

**EMPAT**

| | | | | | | | | | | |
|---|---|---|---|---|---|---|---|---|---|---|
| R | F | F | I | U | E | M | C | A | F | I |
| D | E | S | D | E | N | A | M | S | O | G |
| S | S | S | U | E | A | I | S | W | C | C |
| C | T | X | A | F | L | N | N | S | T | I |
| T | I | G | A | C | N | A | S | A | T | U |
| C | E | H | L | O | L | I | P | E | B | G |
| D | O | N | I | I | Q | M | R | A | X | E |
| R | Z | G | B | Q | E | E | S | O | N | X |
| E | H | M | U | S | T | U | J | U | H | M |
| S | E | P | U | L | U | H | V | O | N | P |
| S | E | E | E | I | X | K | H | M | A | G |

**LIMA**

**TUJUH**

**SEMBILAN**

**ENAM**

**DELAPAN**

**SEPULUH**

50

# OFFERINGS

THE MAJORITY OF BALINESE ARE HINDU. YOU WILL FIND THEIR OFFERINGS EVERYWHERE:
IN FRONT OF A TEMPLE, OUTSIDE A SHOP, EVEN IN THE MIDDLE OF AN INTERSECTION ON THE ROAD.
THESE ARE CALLED CANANG.

HEY! DON'T FORGET THAT IN THE INDONESIAN LANGUAGE A C IS PRONOUNCED CH
    SO IT SOUNDS LIKE THIS... CHANANG.

WHATEVER YOU DO, DON'T EAT THE SWEETS IN AN OFFERING. YOU DON'T WANT TO UPSET THE SPIRITS.

Can you draw your own offerings in here?    51

# WHAT'S IN A NAME?

IN BALI, YOUR NAME INDICATES WHICH NUMBER CHILD YOU ARE.
THE NAMES ARE THE SAME FOR GIRLS AND BOYS.

## HAVE A LOOK AT THE LIST AND TICK WHICH ONE YOU ARE.

☐ IF YOU'RE THE FIRST CHILD YOU HAVE A CHOICE OF GEDE, WAYAN OR PUTU.

☐ IF YOU'RE THE SECOND CHILD YOU CAN CHOOSE FROM MADE OR KADEK.

☐ IF YOU'RE THE THIRD CHILD YOU GET TO CHOOSE FROM NYOMAN, KOMANG.

☐ IF YOU'RE THE FOURTH CHILD YOU CAN CHOOSE THE NAME KETUT.

## AND DO YOU KNOW WHAT?

IF THERE'S MORE THAN FOUR CHILDREN, YOU JUST GO BACK
TO THE BEGINNING AGAIN.

## HERE'S A TIP.

IF YOU WANT TO ASK SOMEBODY THEIR NAME YOU JUST SAY

"SIAPA NAMA ANDA?"

# BALINESE NAMES

| first born | second born | third born | fourth born |
|---|---|---|---|
| GEDE | MADE | NYOMAN | KETUT |
| WAYAN | KADEK | KOMANG | |
| PUTU | | | |

# RICE PADDIES

NYOMAN HAS GOT TO COLLECT HIS LAST BAG OF RICE FROM THE MIDDLE OF HIS RICE PADDY.
CAN YOU HELP HIM GET THERE? watch out for the angry pig, his next door neighbour's bamboo fence and the crazy chicken.

HAVE YOU SEEN SOME AWESOME RICE PADDIES?
SOMETIMES THEY ARE BRILLIANT GREEN AND SOMETIMES THEY CAN BE EXCELLENTLY MUDDY!
can you draw your own rice paddy?

55

# HERE'S IBU GUSTI'S RECIPE FOR HER DELICIOUS NASI GORENG.

ENAK SEKAL!!

## WHAT INGREDIENTS DO YOU NEED?

THIS WILL MAKE ENOUGH FOR ABOUT 4 PEOPLE.

4 CUPS OF COOKED RICE
(make sure it's cool!)

CHICKEN
(about 250 grams)

1 CARROT
(diced really small)

GARLIC
(slice it thin)

1 SHALLOT

½ CABBAGE

VEGETABLE OIL

1 TBS SOY SAUCE

2 TBS KECAP MANIS

CHILLI
(if you like it spicy!)

4 EGGS

## HOW TO COOK IT

ADD THE CHICKEN AND
STIR FRY UNTIL BROWN.

PUT HALF THE OIL INTO
THE WOK AND HEAT.

WHEN IT'S COOKED THROUGH,
TAKE IT OUT AND PUT ASIDE

56

PUT THE OTHER HALF OF THE OIL IN THE WOK.
ADD THE GARLIC AND SHALLOTS
-AND THE CHILLI IF YOU'RE FEELING BRAVE-

AND COOK FOR 2 MINUTES.

ADD THE CARROTS AND CABBAGE
AND COOK TILL NICE AND TENDER.

TIME TO PUT THE NASI
INTO THE NASI GORENG:
ADD THE RICE!

ADD THE CHICKEN.

TIME FOR SOME FLAVOR!
SHAKE IN YOUR KECAP MANIS AND SOY SAUCE
AND STIR FRY UNTIL YUMMY.

FOR AUTHENTIC WARUNG STYLE,
POP A FRIED EGG ON TOP OF EACH SERVING.

NOW THERE'S ONLY ONE THING LEFT TO DO! EAT IT! OR AS WE SAY IN BALI, MAKAN DULU!

# across

- (3) 'TWO' IN BAHASA INDONESIA (3)
- (5) WHITE AND ? - COLOURS OF THE INDONESIAN FLAG (3)
- (6) 'HOUR' IN BAHASA INDONESIA (3)
- (7) CAPITAL OF BALI (8)
- (10) 'SEPULUH' IN ENGLISH (3)
- (11) BALI'S FAVOURITE FOOD - ? GORENG (4)
- (13) 'NO' IN BAHASA INDONESIA (5)
- (14) ? WATU - FAMOUS SURFING SPOT (3)

# down

- (1) INDONESIA'S NATIONAL AIRLINE (6)
- (2) THE CURRENCY OF INDONESIA (6)
- (4) 'BINTANG' IN ENGLISH (4)
- (6) ISLAND TO BALI'S WEST (4)
- (8) BALI'S DAY OF SILENCE (5)
- (9) THE MAIN RELIGION IN BALI (5)
- (12) NGURAH ? AIRPORT (3)

58

# KITES

DURING THE DRY SEASON IN BALI, KIDS AND GROWNUPS LOVE TO FLY KITES.
IT GETS PRETTY CROWDED UP THERE AND **UH HO**! THE STRINGS HAVE BECOME TANGLED.

CAN YOU FOLLOW THE STRING AND MATCH THE KITE TO THE OWNER?

# SHOPPING

WRITE DOWN THE NAMES OF PEOPLE YOU WANT TO BUY PRESENTS FOR AND WHAT YOU THINK THEY WOULD LIKE! YOUR BFF, CRAZY AUNTY, FAVOURITE TEACHER...

🎁 .........................................................................................

..............................................................................................

🎁 .........................................................................................

..............................................................................................

🎁 .........................................................................................

..............................................................................................

🎁 .........................................................................................

..............................................................................................

🎁 .........................................................................................

..............................................................................................

🎁 .........................................................................................

..............................................................................................

# SHOPPING FOR ME!

MAKE A LIST OF THE FAVOURITE THINGS YOU BOUGHT IN BALI.

# MOUNT AGUNG

IF YOU CLIMBED TO THE TOP OF MOUNT AGUNG, YOU WOULD BE AT THE HIGHEST POINT IN BA[...]

IS MOUNT AGUNG?

☐ 2032 metres above sea level
☑ 3142 metres above sea level
☐ 4597 metres above sea level
☐ 5612 metres above sea level

NAME 5 SUPPLIES YOU WOULD BRING TO GET YOU TO THE TOP

1.

2.

3.

4.

5.

62

CAN YOU DRAW YOURSELF ON THE TOP OF THE MOUNTAIN?

# MUSIC

THE TRADITIONAL MUSIC OF BALI IS CALLED THE GAMELAN.
HERE ARE SOME TYPICAL INSTRUMENTS.

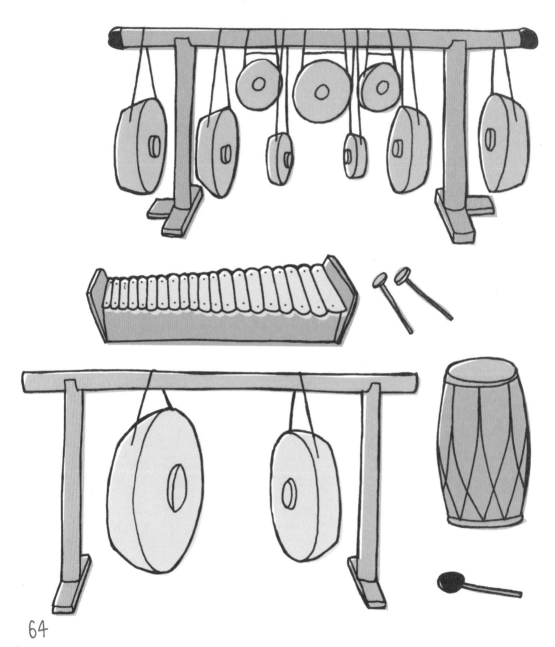

WHAT HAS BEEN THE SOUNDTRACK TO YOUR HOLIDAY?
MAKE A LIST OF THE FAVOURITE SONGS YOU HAVE LISTENED TO.

♫ .................................................................................................

.................................................................................................

♫ .................................................................................................

.................................................................................................

♫ .................................................................................................

.................................................................................................

♫ .................................................................................................

.................................................................................................

♫ .................................................................................................

.................................................................................................

♫ .................................................................................................

.................................................................................................

THESE BEAUTIFUL FRUIT TOWERS ARE CALLED 'GEBOGAN'.

THEY ARE MADE BY BALINESE WOMEN,
WHO CARRY THEM ON THEIR HEADS TO THE TEMPLE.
THEY CAN BE UP TO THREE METRES HIGH!!!

Can you colour in this one?

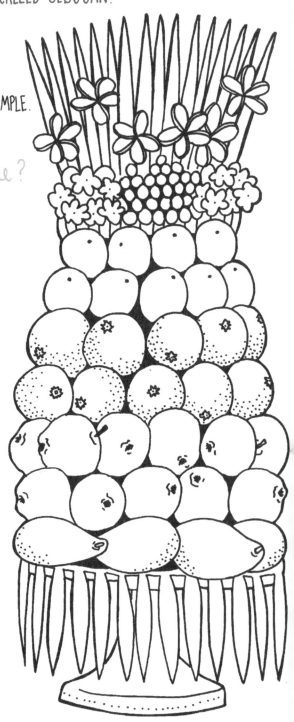

66

CAN YOU MATCH UP THE BAHASA WORD FOR EACH OF THESE ANIMALS?

pig

chicken

dog

cat

fish

cow

bird

monkey

BURUNG

SAPI

MONYET

IKAN

AYAM

ANJING

BABI

KUCING

67

THE RED AND WHITE FLAG OF INDONESIA WAS FIRST RAISED IN 1945 AFTER INDONESIA GAINED INDEPENDENCE.

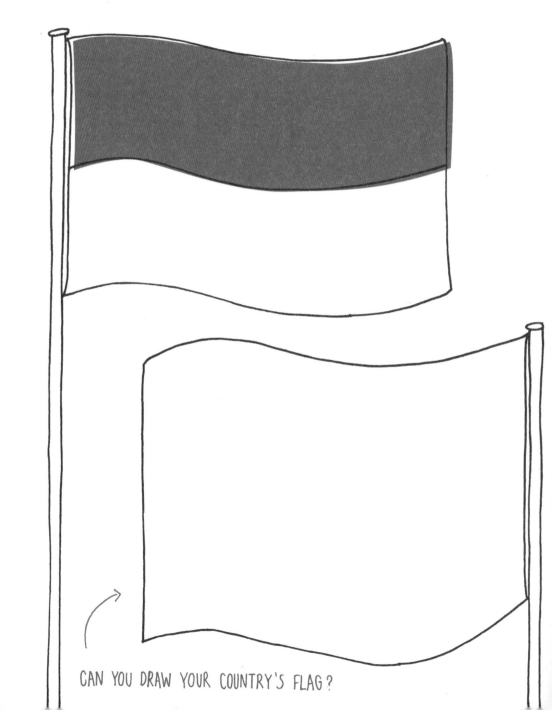

CAN YOU DRAW YOUR COUNTRY'S FLAG?

# CAN YOU UNSCRAMBLE THESE WORDS?
## HERE'S A CLUE... THEY ARE ALL TO DO WITH THE BEACH!

DSAN ................................................................

SFUR ................................................................

USN ................................................................

WEAV ................................................................

TLEOW ................................................................

IIBIKN ................................................................

TAH ................................................................

GEGGOSL ................................................................

FEPPILRS ................................................................

FHIS ................................................................

# CREATE A POSTCARD

BEFORE EMAIL AND SKYPE THERE WERE THESE THINGS CALLED POSTCARDS.
CHECK OUT THE ONE ON THE OTHER PAGE ⟶
have a go designing your own and tell someone about your holiday!

Dear Granny and Grandpa,
Having an AWESOME time in Bali.
I've been surfing, seen lots of temples
and eaten lots of nasi goreng!
Mum and Dad say hi.

Love,
   Putu
(that's my Balinese name)

Granny and Grandpa

1 Wombat Drive

Wombat Town, 2025

The Outback, Australia

# WRITE DOWN THE FAVOURITE PLACES YOU HAVE BEEN TO IN BALI

📍
...................................................................................................

...................................................................................................

📍
...................................................................................................

...................................................................................................

📍
...................................................................................................

...................................................................................................

📍
...................................................................................................

...................................................................................................

📍
...................................................................................................

...................................................................................................

📍
...................................................................................................

...................................................................................................

WRITE DOWN THE MOST AWESOME THINGS YOU HAVE DONE ON YOUR HOLIDAY

- ........................................................................
  ........................................................................
- ........................................................................
  ........................................................................
- ........................................................................
  ........................................................................
- ........................................................................
  ........................................................................
- ........................................................................
  ........................................................................
- ........................................................................
  ........................................................................

# MET ANYONE COOL IN BALI AND WANT TO KEEP IN TOUCH?!
write down their names and email addresses.

☺ ....................................................................................................

@ ....................................................................................................

....................................................................................................

☺ ....................................................................................................

@ ....................................................................................................

....................................................................................................

☺ ....................................................................................................

@ ....................................................................................................

....................................................................................................

☺ ....................................................................................................

@ ....................................................................................................

....................................................................................................

75

# BYE BYE BALI

WHAT TIME IS YOUR PLANE LEAVING? 1:00 am

WHAT IS YOUR FLIGHT NUMBER?

WHAT TIME DO YOU ARRIVE?

HOW ARE YOU GETTING HOME FROM THE AIRPORT? By car

WHO ARE YOU MOST EXCITED ABOUT SEEING? it's ok if it's a pet!

messi

WHAT FOOD ARE YOU LOOKING FORWARD TO EATING?

# WHERE NEXT?!

WOULD YOU LIKE TO COME BACK TO BALI? ☑ yes ☐ no

IS THERE ANYWHERE ELSE IN INDONESIA YOU WANT TO GO?

....................................................................................................

....................................................................................................

....................................................................................................

WHAT ABOUT THE REST OF THE WORLD?
WRITE DOWN ALL THE PLACES YOU WANT TO VISIT NEXT!

....................................................................................................

....................................................................................................

....................................................................................................

....................................................................................................

....................................................................................................

# BEEN THERE, DONE THAT! BAGUS!

STICK IN ANY COOL STUFF: MAYBE AN ENTRY TICKET FROM THE ZOO, A MENU FROM YOUR FAVOURITE RESTAURANT..... ANYTHING TO REMIND YOU OF YOUR AWESOME BALI ADVENTURE. IF YOU FEEL LIKE DRAWING SOME PICTURES, THIS IS THE PERFECT PLACE TO DO IT!

78

# SOLUTIONS NO PEEKING OR CHEATING!

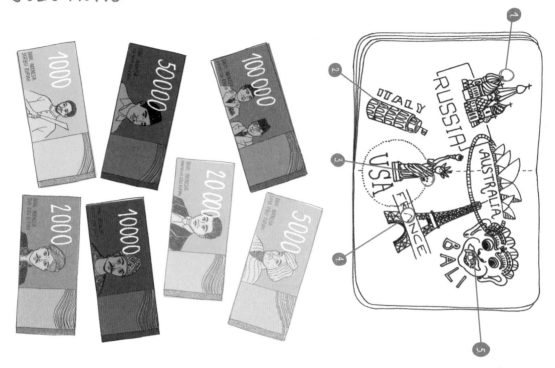

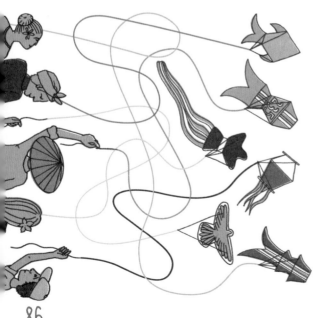

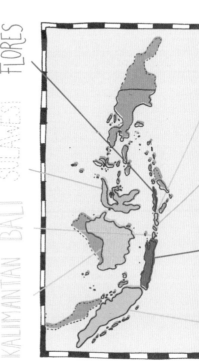

AUGUST IS THE DRIEST MONTH
JANUARY IS THE RAINIEST MONTH

- 24 - 29 degrees celsius
- 29 - 32 degrees celsius
- 32 - 36 degrees celsius

1.
2.
3.
4.
5.

KALIMANTAN   BALI   SULAWESI   FLORES

SUMATRA   JAVA   LOMBOK   SUMBAWA

☐ 2032 metres above sea level

📕 3142 metres above sea level

☐ 4597 metres above sea level

☐ 5612 metres above sea level

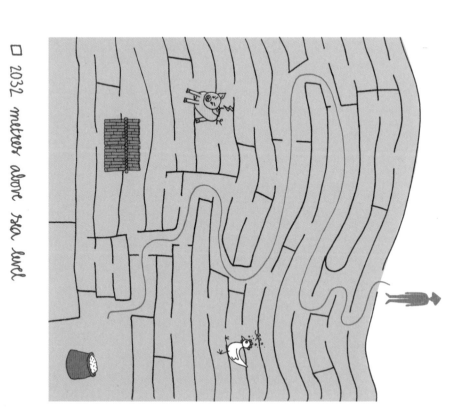

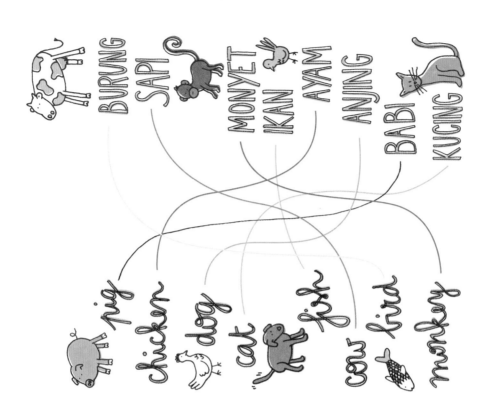

BURUNG
SAPI
MONYET
IKAN
AYAM
ANJING
BABI
KUCING

pig
chicken
dog
cat
fish
cow
bird
monkey

SAND
SURF
SUN
WAVE
TOWEL
BIKINI
HAT
GOGGLES
FLIPPERS
FISH

DSAN
SFUR
USN
WEAV
TLEOW
IIBIKN
TAH
GEGGOSL
FEPPILRS
FHIS